LONDINIUM REVISITED

OLLI TOOLEY

Other titles by the same author.

- Time Tunnel to Londinium
- Time Tunnel at the Seaside

LONDINIUM REVISITED

OLLI TOOLEY

ISBN-10: 1530891760

ISBN-13: 978-1530891764

DEDICATION

For my son, Morton, who took a sudden interest in Latin, for no apparent reason.

NOTE

I began this book in 2011 but then didn't do anything with it until 2015. So the action takes place in a fictional version of London, loosely based on the real London of around 2011.

CONTENTS

ACKNOWLEDGMENTS

The contributors to the forums at www.unrv.com for their help, especially 'Nephele' for help with names. Any historical accuracy can be attributed to them and any inaccuracies can only be blamed on me.

The contributors of www.latindiscussion.com forums for their help with Latin words and phrases. Again all credit must go to them for good Latin, and all blame for bad Latin goes to me.

My sister Sarah, who is an English teacher, for proof reading.

Teachers in general. They are appallingly undervalued and should be paid more than sports stars or politicians.

To my kids, for listening to the story and telling me what bits were boring or too hard to understand. Nobody knows what children like better than children themselves.

Lastly my Latin master, Mr. Wolfson, who tried in vain to teach me any Latin. Mea culpa, mea maxima culpa.

I
LIVING IN THE PAST

The early morning sun streamed through the bedroom window making the dust particles dance in celebration of the new day. The sunbeam painted a bright rhombus onto a faded 'Harry Potter' duvet on the bed.

Under the duvet with his face covered by a book, lay David Johnson, snoring loudly, the pages stuck to his face. The book was titled 'Lingua Latina per se Illustrata' and was written entirely in Latin. David had decided to learn Latin.

Most ten year old boys want to learn cheat codes for games on the latest console, but David was struggling with declensions and conjugations instead. There was a very good reason for this however. He had just recently had an adventure in which he found himself transported back in time to Roman Londinium. He had made a new friend called Marcus, and learned all sorts of stuff.

Marcus only spoke Latin and he had taught David quite a few words. David found himself interested in learning more, although it looked as if he would never be able to go back again. The hole in the wall that he had crawled through had been very securely bricked up.

It turned out that David had a particular gift for learning languages. He was far better at learning them than most children his age. The school he went to was in inner London, and most of the children there spoke another language as well as English. David could converse fairly well in Polish, Urdu, Arabic and Romanian. In fact his best friend Andrei was Romanian, and David enjoyed going round to his house speaking only Romanian with his parents, even though both of them had a good grasp of English.

David rolled over and the book clattered to the floor. He pulled the old duvet over his tousled blonde hair and continued dozing. It was about five in the morning so he didn't have to get up for a few hours yet.

~ ~ ~ ~ ~ ~ ~ ~ ~ ~ ~

Only a few miles away, but about one thousand eight hundred years earlier, a man stood watching work progress on the building of a wall. His name was Marcus Septimus

Faber, and he was experienced at large building projects. The wall was close to completion and he was checking off jobs on a wax tablet with the centurion of the legion working on the building. Marcus had served in the army and risen to the rank of centurion. Now he was an old man, into his sixties, and a civilian; but his skills and experience as a builder and architect were much needed for large projects, such as this new wall around Londinium.

Two miles long, twenty feet high and eight feet thick, the wall incorporated two sides of the military fort in the north west of the city and had five gateways with roads leading to every part of the country. This one led North-East towards Camulodunum, once the most important town in Britain.

~ ~ ~ ~ ~ ~ ~ ~ ~ ~ ~

David's mum called upstairs. “David! School! Get up!”

David rolled over and fell out of bed. He woke up pretty quickly after that. He stretched and yawned and found a shirt under his bed. Then he stumped downstairs.

“You can't wear that shirt David it's got tomato sauce over it.”

David made a noise that could not be deciphered but sounded like “mmphrphrghmph”

“Here, put this one on, it's a bit big on you

but at least it's clean. And get some breakfast down you. You've got to be in early today, remember?"

David's school was very keen on school outings. This year their class had been on a trip to London Zoo, the Olympic park visitor centre, the Thames flood barrier and, most recently, the Museum of London, where they got an unexpected opportunity to search for buried treasure. That was when David became a minor celebrity by finding some Roman coins.

Today they were going to the Tower Of London. David was really looking forward to it because he had learned that they had a huge collection of weapons and armour from throughout history.

Absently, he picked up his mum's locket. She had let him keep it as he got very upset when she tried to take it back. It was this locket which had saved him from an awkward situation when he had travelled back in time, and he now kept it with him all the time.

David's mum dropped him off at the school gates. She didn't come in, or bother about a hug, because she knew David didn't want her making a fuss when his friends were around.

The first part of the journey was uneventful. They walked to Whitechapel underground station, and it was only two stops on the district line to Tower Hill station. They came out of the station on the wrong side of the road, although Mrs. O'Keefe said this was so that they could see a preserved section of London Wall there.

The class then made their way down some steps to a subway that would bring them out on the other side of the busy road, right by the Tower of London, but David was distracted by something shiny over by some bushes. Thinking it might be some buried treasure, he went over and bent down to have a closer look. There was something metallic, but most of it was buried in the soil. David pulled on it. It turned out to be a small aluminium spirit level, just a few inches long. David put it in his pocket and looked round; but by then the rest of the class had moved on and, unusually, the classroom assistant hadn't noticed that David wasn't with them.

David decided he could catch up with them easily enough but then his attention was caught again by the wall itself. There was a paved area in front of the wall, with a bronze statue standing on a low plinth. On the plinth was a metal plate which bore the words 'STATUE BELIEVED TO BE THE ROMAN EMPEROR TRAJAN'. Behind the statue was an area of well-kept lawn. He walked across the grass and touched the rough stone of the wall, running his fingers over it. As he did so he thought about his friend Marcus who he would never see again, since the hole he had crawled through had been properly sealed up.

"Oi, you! Get away from that!" A man was shouting at David. He looked like some sort of security guard.

He was hurrying over, but David decided not to hang around. The ancient wall formed a narrow angle with a modern concrete wall, and David managed to scramble up between the rough Roman masonry on one side, and the textured concrete on the other. He clambered over the modern wall and dashed away past the station on his right. Without really thinking, he raced along a brick paved road, with a few taxis waiting by the kerb.

He wasn't really being sensible as he had not been doing anything wrong, but he didn't think he would be able to explain to the man who had shouted at him. It just seemed easier to run away, find his way back to the rest of the class, and just blend in. He carried on for a little way until there was a turning. He turned right, and right again at the next junction, hoping to get back to where he was supposed to be, but instead he ended up getting himself lost.

II
THICK AS A BRICK

David was lost, and not sure which way he should go.

He was looking around him and walking in no particular direction, when he bumped into two older boys, who should have been in school but weren't.

"Oi you, watch where you're goin'." said one.

"Yeah, you little toe-rag." added the other.

"Sorry." replied David.

But it was clear that the two boys were just out looking for trouble. One of them grabbed David by the arms and pushed him against a wall. He had hold of David's coat sleeve, and David was just able to wriggle out of his coat and get away as the boy punched the wall where David's head had been only a moment before.

"Ow! You little ...." the boy yelled, and then

the pair gave chase, running after David.

David ran blindly, fear gave him speed he never knew he had. He dodged past office workers on their way to work. Unfortunately, in his panic, it didn't occur to him to ask them for help. He dashed out across a busy road, forcing taxis and cars to screech to a halt. The two boys chasing him bumped into people, and then had to stop as the angry drivers continued on their way.

David chanced a brief glance over his shoulder and, seeing that he had put a fair distance between himself and the boys, sprinted to the next junction, where he turned left. Dashing for the next corner he turned right, hoping that they would not see which way he turned. He chose to turn right, and then took a left fork almost immediately afterwards. Another right took him onto a road which, he had time to notice, was called Fenchurch Street. He was out of breath now and slowed down a bit as he walked along, glancing behind him every now and then.

A little further on there was an old church, and, David realised, he could see the 'Gherkin'. It was shining in the morning sun as he looked to his left.

In front of him was a building with a large colourful coat of arms, and directly in front of him was a low wall and iron railings. On the wall was a large plaque with information about London Wall and Aldgate. There was a drawing of the gatehouse with two large square towers over the top of two arches and the wall itself stretching away on either side. It looked much bigger than he had really imagined. It wasn't just a gate but a small castle with rows of windows that clearly looked out from rooms. Several people could have lived in the gatehouse. Indeed, the plaque informed David that a famous man called Geoffrey Chaucer had lived there from 1374.

Suddenly he heard a shout from behind him, and he realised the two boys had come a different way and spotted him.

He dashed quickly past the church and round to the right, following round to the other side of the church, past some sort of fence, and then realised he was in a narrow dead end with walls on both sides. If the boys followed him here, he was trapped. There was evidence of fallen masonry, presumably from the recent earthquake, and a hole in the wall near the ground. There was a faint glow coming from the hole. David remembered a similar glow from a hole that he had crawled through before. That had taken him to Roman Londinium, but he had no idea if this would take him to the same place and time. He hoped that he might see his friend Marcus, but what if the hole led him to the age of the dinosaurs? Besides, it didn't look possible for him to squeeze through. A shout at the other end of the alley left him with no choice but to try. He pulled away a brick that was loose and squeezed into the gap. He got his head through, scrabbling at loose bricks, then wriggling and pulling his stomach tight, he dragged his foot clear just as the boy caught his shoe, which came off. He was scratched and bruised and had only one shoe, but he felt sure the boys would not be able to follow him here, wherever he was.

III
ALIVE AND WELL AND LIVING IN

As he looked around, David was a little surprised to find that he wasn't in a narrow built up area, but was in fact in the open. The smells were different too, instead of the dusty smell of grimy buildings and traffic fumes, there was a smell of countryside, and animals. The constant thrum of traffic was gone. Instead there was a silence, broken by a cockerel crowing. At least it was hot and sunny.

David was scratched and bruised, but not badly hurt. He stood up and then looked up into the face of a fully armed Roman legionary.

"Ah-way." said David, with confidence, but the legionary was in no mood to talk. He grabbed David by the arm, and dragged him away.

There was much activity going on, with citizens going about their business. Close by, a huge wall was being worked on. There was also a gateway in the wall. David recognised the building although it bore almost no resemblance to the drawing he had just been looking at. This was 'Aldgate' as built by the Romans. The building was still under construction with all sorts of workmen, their tunics tucked into belts, carrying tools that marked them out as carpenters, stone masons, and other tradesmen.

They approached a temporary shelter just inside the gateway where more soldiers stood on guard and David was thrust inside, where he fell on his face.

He looked up just enough to see a man with a weathered face. His hair, greying around the temples, swept across his balding head in a sideways comb-over. He wore the simple tunic of a working Roman, but the red stripes down each side indicated his rank. David noticed that he was straining to look at some sort of document on the table in front of him, his face close to the paper, his eyes half closed, making the lines on his face stand out. 'He must have bad eyesight', thought David.

The legionary spoke rapidly and David could make out enough to realise that his presence was being explained to the man behind the table. Then the man spoke.

"Surgay puer!" It was a commanding voice, yet at the same time gentle.

David searched his brain trying to think of the meaning of the words, and felt pretty sure he was being told to stand up. For confirmation, the legionary placed a hand under his arm and dragged him upright, where he looked into the puzzled, but fairly friendly face of the man. There was a flicker of recognition on the face, which passed briefly.

"Quisnam es tu, puer?" the man asked

David knew this one; 'what is your name, boy?'

"Day-wi-dus." he replied smartly.

Again the man's face was creased with a puzzled expression, but this passed after a moment.

He muttered something and shook his head as if to clear some strange thought that was lodged there.

David remembered the importance of the Roman bulla, and how his mum's locket had impressed his friend, Marcus, when he had been in this situation before. He pulled the little gold chain from his pocket, with the locket dangling from it, and held it out for inspection to the man, adding for clarification,

"Ecce, mea bulla."

At this, the man's eyes widened,

"Day-wi-dus?" he gasped.

"Vero, Day-wi-dus." David clutched at the word 'vero' meaning truly, but he had not yet begun to form the idea that this old man might be his friend Marcus.

Marcus was also having some difficulty getting the facts to fit with what he knew. He had last seen David fifty years earlier when they were both boys, but now he was an old man and his friend was still the same age. Thinking hard, he realised that there were stories told in this island of people who went to visit the land of the gods and returned after only a few hours or days to find that time had passed many years in the real world. He presumed this must be what had happened. He knew that Day-wi-dus was no ordinary boy. The last time they had met, he had somehow managed to recover Marcus' bulla from the deepest part of the river. He must have direct access to the gods themselves.

He called for a slave and spoke to him briefly. David recognised the words for water and wine and hoped that there would be more of the former. Shortly afterwards, the slave returned with jugs of water and wine as David had expected, and he was allowed to pour his own drink while the man watched him with a puzzled expression.

Soon, another man came in and looked at David. He had a leather bag, and wore a toga.

Something about the way he investigated David's minor cuts and bruises suggested that he was some kind of a doctor, and this was confirmed when he began to pour an acrid smelling liquid onto a wad of linen, and proceeded to wipe the stinging liquid onto the cuts. The smell wafting into David's nostrils reminded him strongly of fish and chips. He gritted his teeth and tried not to wince, as everybody knew that stinging made cuts better, and he wasn't going to be a baby in front of these Romans.

After the treatment he did add a little wine to his water.

"Vere, tu es Daywidus?" asked the man Are you truly David?

"Sum" replied David. I am

"Nomen mihi Marcus Septimus Faber. Amicus tuus Marcus." Explained the man.

David understood the words. 'My name is Marcus Septimus Faber. Your friend Marcus.' But his face showed disbelief and confusion.

Still speaking in Latin, Marcus added,

"You brought back my bulla, when it fell into the river."

David still looked disbelieving, then Marcus reached into a small leather pouch and produced a small glass marble. David's eyes widened as he recognised one of the marbles that he had given to Marcus just a few weeks earlier. At least, as far as he had experienced time it had only been weeks. For Marcus, it had been half a century. David frowned. He looked at the lined face, and the calloused hands of his friend.

Marcus spoke again.

“You have been to the land of the Gods. You may think you were gone for a few days but it is fifty years since the last time we met. What was it like there?”

David's mind was racing, trying to fit the conversation into some framework that made sense. The entire conversation was, of course, still in Latin. David could just about understand the words but not the ideas, and there were questions that David could not ask because he simply did not know enough words to ask them. He was trying to think of something sensible to say, when they were interrupted.

IV
SO MUCH TROUBLE

The shelter they were in was a sort of tent, but not really like any tent David had seen. It was large enough to stand up in, and shaped very much like a small house. There were poles at the front and back that supported the top of the roof and another pole went along the ridge between the two supporting poles. The material it was made of was thick and stiff and smelled like his mum's leather jacket that she never wore, but never threw away. Outside, although David hadn't had time to notice this, there were ropes fastened to the ground that pulled the roof out to form the slope. If David had ever been in the scouts, he might possibly have seen tents that were similar but made of green canvas.

Outside the tent there was a bit of a

commotion. The cause of this was soon obvious, as the legionary who had brought David here, now also brought two other boys, both shouting, and struggling ineffectually in the soldier's tight grip.

He threw them to the ground inside the tent, as he had done with David, and spoke rapidly to Marcus.

David was very worried, he knew about time travel paradoxes and he knew that they must not do anything to upset history, because if they did, then there might not be a future to go back to. He had thought long and hard about bringing Marcus' bulla back to him during his previous adventures, but felt that the events of a young boy's life could surely not impinge much on the course of history, however he simply didn't know if these two bullies would have enough sense to keep their mouths shut and not blab to people when they got back to their own time. When they got back? If they got back! What if the Romans decided to imprison them, or beat them so badly they died? In learning Latin, David had also learned a lot about Roman ways and he knew that violence and death were quite commonplace, even for the rich and powerful.

"Non hostis." David said, trying to convey to Marcus that the boys were not enemies, then he added "Non nocere" which he had picked up from the Hippocratic Oath 'Primum non nocere' which means 'First, do no harm'.

Speaking quickly to the two boys David said,

"Don't do anything stupid and we might all get out of this in one piece"

Marcus looked first at David, and then asked the boys their names. David translated for the boys who responded with "Cameron" and "Alex", muttered with a mixture of fear and irritation.

Hoping to take the initiative, David spoke. Searching for the right words, he fell back on a mix of Romanian and Latin

"Le tremite terra Deorum .... Deorum irati", it was his best attempt at saying 'Send them back to the land of the Gods, the Gods are angry'.

It appeared to have made enough sense to Marcus who knew that David was only learning Latin. When they had first met, David could not say 'hello' properly pronouncing it 'Aah-vay' instead of 'Aah-way', and after that, Marcus had needed to teach him everything. But David had learned quickly, and he also had secret powers. He could take a small stick and make a flame grow from it, just by striking it along a rough surface, and he had produced items of rare beauty, such as small glass spheres in sparkling colours.

Most importantly David had somehow

managed to reach to the bottom of the river in Londinium and recover Marcus' bulla, returning it to him. That fact alone meant that Marcus felt he owed a debt to David, and he would take his words seriously for fear of upsetting the mysterious Celtic Gods who still held a great deal of sway in these Islands, even though the Roman Gods were, of course, superior.

"Quid ergo faciemus?" he said to David. 'What should we do?'

"Le remittite." 'Send them back.' replied David drawing on everything he had read, remembering a word in Latin which was similar to the Romanian word he had used earlier, 'tremite'. The word "le" wasn't necessary but it didn't matter.

Marcus understood and gave orders for the legionary to take hold of the boys and follow him. David went with them and urgently explained to Cameron and Alex that there was nothing to worry about but that they must not breathe a word to anyone when they got back to London.

"What-choo on about?" responded Alex angrily, "I'm gonna get you, an' this lot. We'll come back 'ere wiv a copper and get you for this."

"Yeah!" added Cameron, "You'll pay for this."

David looked panicked, if he allowed them

to be sent back and they told the police, there might be hordes of people from the 21st century coming through the gap and into Roman Londinium. If he let them stay in Roman Londinium, there was no end to the number of ways they could change history.

David tried to imagine modern soldiers coming through the time tunnel, armed with modern weapons. Ancient Roman shields and iron spears against assault rifles? It didn't bear thinking about. He wasn't at all sure if it was possible for someone to kill their own ancestor. That was the famous time travel paradox. If you went back in time and killed your grandfather, then you might never be born and then you could not go back in time. The situation was impossible, but what about other things, like changing the past in small ways, and as a result changing the course of history? What if the Roman Empire collapsed earlier than it actually did? Or splintered into a Northern and Southern empire, the north controlled by Britons armed with captured guns and a limited supply of ammunition? David's mind was racing ahead of the situation.

He pleaded again with Alex and Cameron not to say anything, and then they reached the gap in the wall where David had seen the legionary earlier. It was just a large rock on a grassy bank with a deep hole in the soil underneath. It looked like the sort of place where a small animal might try to hide from a predator, or where a small person could shelter from the rain. Nothing more.

With David still imploring the boys not to say anything, they were pushed by the centurion into the gap, which looked too small to accommodate one of them properly, never mind both; yet the two boys scrabbled through a narrow gap and completely disappeared from 2nd century Londinium, emerging seconds later in 21st century London.

V
A TIME FOR EVERYTHING

Alex and Cameron headed off quickly in search of somebody to tell about what had happened and soon came across a pair of police officers. The boys began to give a hasty and confused account of travelling back in time, and being beaten up by Roman soldiers, before the officers began to ask them just why they were not in school. It didn't take long before the two boys were being escorted to the police station and various phone calls to parents and school were being made. Instead of putting the whole of history in doubt, they had just got themselves into a whole lot of trouble.

~ ~ ~ ~ ~ ~ ~ ~ ~ ~ ~

Meanwhile in 2nd century Londinium, David really needed to go to the toilet, having drunk quite a bit of watered down wine earlier.

He knew that Roman latrines were different from those in the 21st century because he had used one when he visited Marcus' villa on his previous visit. The main difference was that they didn't use toilet paper, but instead had a sponge on a stick which was dipped in water to clean it after use. It was a bit like using a toilet brush on yourself instead of cleaning the toilet with it. Luckily David had not needed to use it.

Even so, the latrine that David was shown to this time, after going through a bit of miming to get Marcus to understand what he needed, was a bit daunting. The last time had been in Marcus' family villa. It was a small room with a door, and a simple wooden bench with a hole cut in it. This was a temporary public latrine, built for the tradesmen and soldiers involved in constructing the wall. It was just outside the wall, where a stream flowed past towards the River Thames. Over this stream, there was a large rectangular tent. Inside there was a long wooden bench with holes in it at regular intervals. The stream ran along underneath the bench. Seated at various points along this bench were a number of soldiers, all doing their business.

David felt the urge to turn around and walk straight out but he also really needed to go, and felt himself redden deeply as he chose a seat as far from anyone else as he could manage. He was wearing trousers and felt like a complete idiot as he pulled them down just far enough. At least his shirt was extra long and baggy. Standing was clearly out of the question, and he was eternally grateful when he had finished and could get out of there and as far away as possible.

Soon after this he said goodbye to Marcus and returned to the time tunnel, crawling back to the 21st Century. He was thankful to be able to retrieve his shoe, and quickly headed back in what he supposed was the direction of the Tower of London. On the way however he was distracted once again, this time by a lively demonstration that appeared to be taking place near what looked like a building site.

A small but determined group of people were holding placards with slogans like.

"DON'T BURY OUR HISTORY"

"INFORMATION NOT DESECRATION"

"MORE TIME TO DIG"

They were a mixed bunch, some were young, dressed casually in jeans and colourful shirts, but some wore suits and were obviously older. Then David noticed a familiar figure. It was the curator of artifacts from the Museum of London. David had met him on the previous school trip and he had also been on the television talking about David's amazing discovery of Roman coins.

"Hello" said David, "What's going on?"

The curator took in David's disheveled appearance, but was too interested in his own topic to comment about that.

"Developers want to put a building on this site which was demolished by the earthquake. But we think there may be a Roman building of some importance under the surface and we need time to investigate properly." explained the curator. "They plan to level the site and lay foundations in less than a week, which will mean any archaeology will be buried once again, perhaps forever."

David was very interested in archaeology because, not long ago, he had been on an archaeological dig and had become a minor celebrity after finding some Roman coins. In fact the coins had been in his pocket and he had pretended to find them; but it was the same thing, more or less.

"So that's what the protest is about then?" he asked the curator.

"Yes, we've tried to explain to the contractors how important this is, but they talk as if the only thing that matters is money, and getting this building up as soon as possible. They won't even let us into the site because they say it is dangerous, but we know that's just an excuse. Tell people it's a health and safety issue and nobody questions it. All we need is a week, to do some geophysical surveys and put in a few trenches to do some investigating. If we find anything of value then we can apply for an extension to investigate more."

David knew all about geophysical surveys from watching 'Time Team' on television. They could tell where to dig, based on readings taken on the ground before they even picked up a shovel.

The curator suddenly changed the subject.

“Shouldn't you be in school?” he asked

“I'm supposed to be on a school trip.” David replied. “I got separated from the group and ran into a spot of bother. I should be at the Tower of London.”

“Right, well you're in luck.” said the curator. I've still got your teacher's mobile number in my phone from the school trip you did with us. We decided to swap numbers so we could keep in touch, in case of problems when we were digging down by the Thames.”

The curator referred to his address book.

“There she is, Mrs. O'Keefe.” he added, as he hit the call button.

It goes without saying that, when a very worried and angry Mrs. O'Keefe arrived, she did a good deal of stern talking, David did a good deal of shoe gazing and mumbling apologies, and the curator did a good deal of placating and excusing. Eventually David was back with the rest of his class, having missed quite a lot of the best bits, the best bits being the bits with weapons and gory stories about the bloodier bits of history.

As they were whisked, rapidly, on a moving walkway, past the glittering 'Crown Jewels' encased behind thick glass, David's thoughts turned to his friend, the museum curator. If there was some way that David could make sure they found something really interesting on the building site, they would surely be allowed longer to dig there.

That night he spent a lot of time on the internet on a Latin language discussion forum, getting Latin translations for a variety of phrases that he thought he might need. He wrote each of these phrases out in a small notebook so that he wouldn't have to rely on just his own knowledge of Latin.

He also picked up a compass and a pedometer and stuffed them into a small bag together with the notebook, a pencil and the little spirit level that he had found yesterday.

VI
PLAY IN TIME

The next day was Saturday, and David already had a plan. He woke up early enough to be eating breakfast with his mother. This was already surprising enough, but then he got ready to go out without being asked, and suggested going to his Nan's house for a bit.

This was a simple, yet brilliant part of his plan, because his Nan lived within a very short walk of the Tower of London. He would go there first, and then make an excuse to get away so he could go back to the time tunnel.

David's Nan was a typical 'little-old-lady' with almost white hair and big glasses. David was already taller than her, even when she made a point of standing up straight. But she had a good sense of fun. She also had a big metal tin which always had toffees and other nice things inside.

Her small and neat flat was decorated in an old fashioned style, the wallpaper was in shades of brown and orange featuring huge unrealistic flowers and leaves. The carpet was a similar colour scheme with a deep pile, although well worn. Everything in the flat was old and worn but of very good quality, and that included David's Nan.

After enjoying some toffees, and filling his Nan in on recent events, he admitted that he had only popped over because he had to go somewhere for his mum and it was on the way. Before going, however, he made sure to ask if there was anything his Nan needed him to do.

"Oh, yes, now you mention it. I knocked my spare glasses down the back of the sideboard yesterday." she told him.

"No problem, Nan." David said, and immediately he was face down on the floor reaching underneath the sideboard, feeling for the glasses. His Nan was sprightly for her age but she certainly couldn't get down on the floor and squeeze under the furniture like David could.

"Got them, Nan." said a jubilant David as he got up with the spare glasses in hand.

"Oh, thank you, David." said his Nan, "I don't really need them to be honest. They're just cheap reading glasses, but I don't like them being out of place."

Suddenly David had an idea. “Nan, could I possibly have those glasses. There's a man I know who really needs a pair of reading glasses but he can't afford them.”

David's Nan smiled, “You're such a thoughtful lad, David, of course you can take them. If I really need another pair I can afford them. You'd better have another toffee, as a reward, to see you on your way.” added his Nan, with a twinkle in her eye.

Once outside, David sprinted off towards the Tower of London, slowing down as he got out of breath, and jogging most of the way to Aldgate. Once he was by the plaque, showing where the gatehouse had once stood, he took out the compass and pedometer and walked the distance to the building site where the protesters wanted to carry out an archaeological dig. He made several notes in his notebook, and as soon as he was done, he headed for the alleyway next to the church, where he could wriggle through the hole in the wall into Roman Londinium once more.

On the other side of the Time Tunnel he headed straight for the tent where he had met Marcus earlier. The legionary standing outside the tent recognised David and stood aside without a word. He knew that this boy was favoured by the gods. Inside Marcus was, once again, struggling to read a document.

"The Gods have a task for you." David said, employing one of the phrases he had got from the Latin language forum on the internet, the night before.

"The Gods need you to bury a gift for them in the ground. I can show you where, but you must find the items that they need. They have sent me with a gift for you in exchange"

"What items do they need?" asked Marcus.

"Coins, small things, ordinary things, lots of different things, in a lead box."

"What is the gift from the gods?"

David took the reading glasses from his pocket.

"You must keep these a secret from other mortals." he insisted.

David put the glasses on his face to show how they were worn, and then handed them to Marcus, who put the glasses on as David had demonstrated. David pointed at the document that Marcus had been struggling to read. There was a brief moment when David wasn't at all sure if his plan had worked, but then Marcus' face creased into a smile as he realised he was able to read the writing without any trouble at all.

Marcus took the glasses off and put them into a pouch before calling a legionary into the tent. He fired off a series of instructions to the soldier, who departed with purpose.

It was not more than a few minutes before some items were being brought into the tent. The tricky part was a lead box, but it didn't take long for one of the tradesmen to cover a simple wooden box with lead sheeting. This was brought to the tent, and David picked various items from those on offer and placed them inside the box. He put the lid on and asked that everyone should leave except for Marcus.

Once the rest of the people had gone, David went to the gate house and took out his compass and pedometer. Referring to his notes, he paced away from the gate-house to a place which, by his calculations, should be roughly in the middle of the building site where the archaeologists wanted to dig. It was a short distance outside the wall, and not far from the public latrine that he had used. With Marcus' help they buried the lead box a few feet under the soil and covered it over.

"The gods say this must not be disturbed." advised David, and Marcus nodded his assent.

Then they went back to the time tunnel where David said goodbye once again to Marcus. He wondered if this would be the last time they met. Marcus looked old, and David wondered how long Romans usually lived.

As a last parting gift he reached into his pocket and pulled out the little spirit level and showed it to Marcus. Once Marcus had the idea of it, David told him he could keep it, but must also keep it a secret from other mortals.

VII
BACK TO THE FAMILY

Once back in modern day London, David raced home as quickly as possible. When he arrived home breathless and later than his mum expected, he had to apologise, and made some excuse about meeting a friend and losing track of the time.

He made himself useful, helping get plates out for dinner, running to the shop for milk at the last minute, and clearing the table. He even helped a bit with the washing up, so his mum wasn't really surprised when he asked for a favour. What did surprise her was that he asked to go back to the Museum of London.

David had recently turned his school life around. He had always been intelligent, but was easily distracted, and his insatiable curiosity kept getting him into trouble. But just lately his interest and natural gift in languages had amazed his teachers, and he was getting top marks in history. Even in maths and English he was getting on better, perhaps because he was now a minor celebrity.

So, on Sunday morning David and his mum got the bus into the City to visit the Museum of London. As soon as they got to the Roman London exhibits, David sought out his friend the museum curator. After introducing his mum, he got straight down to his plan.

"If we can get 'Time Team' involved in the demand to carry out an archaeological dig at that building site do you think that would help us?"

The curator smiled the smile of an adult who knows that the grand schemes of a child are not really practical.

"Alas, I doubt if we can get them involved in time. The developers want to start laying foundations in just over a week. It's 'Catch 22', if we don't find evidence of important archaeology on the site, we can't dig, and if we can't dig, then we can't find evidence." explained the curator.

"What about a geophysical survey?" asked David.

"They won't let us onto the site to carry one out. It really is a tricky situation."

David was pretty disappointed, in fact he was downright annoyed. He had gone to a lot of trouble to plant something that would be easy to find using metal detectors, and would have a good chance of surviving burial for one thousand eight hundred years. He had taken his Nan's glasses, and a great many risks, for a plan that really had no chance of success. If only he could think of some way to get Channel 4 to take an interest.

They spent quite a bit of time looking around the museum. David's mum knew a fair bit herself but was pleased to find that David knew a great deal that was new to her. There was a scale model of Roman Londinium and it amused her to hear David explain how certain parts were not quite right, there was a building that he assured her was not there, and other buildings which he insisted should have been present but were missing. Nevertheless, his heart wasn't really in it and she could tell he wasn't happy about the situation.

Back at home that evening, David sat with a cup of hot chocolate and watched a repeat of 'Time Team', where they were digging up a Roman villa. Then on the news there was the usual boring stuff and he thumbed through a book about Julius Caesar, although he half heard an item about a petition being handed in to the Prime Minister at 10 Downing Street.

Later, before falling asleep he began to wonder if he could get a petition and hand it in to the Prime Minister. As he slept, he dreamed about walking through the gates at the entrance to Downing Street carrying a pile of signatures. As he walked, the pile got bigger and bigger, and the street got longer and longer. He was exhausted by the time he reached the great black door guarded by two policemen.

The door was huge, the policemen were huge. They were towering over David, who was shrinking smaller and smaller, as the petition got heavier and heavier, until he was buried under the weight of paper. Then the Prime Minister lifted the papers off him and said

"Why have you brought this to me? I am not an archaeologist. You should have taken this to Channel 4 studios, David. ... David! ... David!!"

"... David!" called his mum, come on you'll be late for school, you've been doing really well lately, you don't want to spoil it do you? It's the last week of term as well."

YES! Only one more week to go, but so much to do. He leapt out of bed, and was dressed and ready to go in a matter of minutes. He ran into school and straight to his classroom, where Mrs. O'Keefe was just taking chairs down off the desks. He helped her finish the job, all the while explaining his plan to get all the kids in school to write to Channel 4 and demand that the ‘Time Team’ crew send someone to the building site to consider the possibility of filming an episode there. He explained why it was so important, because the site could have some very valuable material but that developers would be building over it in a week.

Mrs. O'Keefe seemed to like the idea, she said it could be a class project for everyone to write a letter and explain why it was so important not to bury our past. They had a whole lesson about archaeology and came up with lots of ideas for what to write in the letters. During lunch Mrs. O'Keefe discussed the letters with the head-teacher, who was always keen on getting the children involved with campaigns and learning about the world beyond the school gates, hence all the school trips.

By the end of the school day, every class in the school had begun writing letters to

Time Team
c/o Channel 4
124 Horseferry Road,
London
SW1P 2TX

Dear Tony Robinson and the Time Team,

... etc.

By the next day, they had a big pile of letters written by nearly three hundred pupils, as well as one or two written by members of staff. The head-teacher had already been in contact with the production team at Channel 4. She had also spoken to a friend of hers who, by happy coincidence, worked for the local newspaper. She already knew about David, having covered the story of his archaeological find, so she was keen to cover this story as well.

With permission from David's mum, David and a small group headed to Victoria, in south-west London as soon as school was over. The group included the head-teacher and her friend from the local paper, a photographer who introduced himself as Bill, Mrs. O'Keefe, and of course David. They took a taxi from Victoria station. They took photos of them getting out of the cab, and going into the grand, curved-glass fronted, building on the corner of Horseferry Road. He was fascinated by walking over the circular glass floor at the front, and peering down to the floor below.

Inside reception, they were met by a producer who worked on the programme, and she asked David a few questions about the site. She was fascinated to hear about David's previous discovery of Roman coins, and thought it was a great idea to check out the building site, although she warned him that it might not be possible. With that, a few pleasantries exchanged, and a bag containing various Channel 4 badges and such like being given to the group, they headed back to the East End of London.

VIII
A WEEK OF MOMENTS

The next morning was Wednesday, and David went to school feeling rather deflated. He didn't know what he expected, marching bands? A parade of archaeologists down Mile End Road? Professors shaking his hand and weeping thanks? He hadn't done anything really, other than get a lot of kids to ask some adults to make other adults do the right thing. Nothing would come of it, and the building site would be concreted over and a new building would go up there, perhaps like the Channel 4 headquarters, all steel and glass; he liked it, but he also liked the rows of creamy marble pillars and ornate statues. Nobody he knew could ever hope to understand the beauty of those statues all painted and gilded, glinting in the Londinium sunshine, but he had seen them. He had seen the Romano-British ladies in long flowing gowns of vibrant colours, the legionaries in gleaming bronze and steel. He had seen the river Thames, wider than it is now, spanned by a single bridge, and the wall, so huge and majestic. He could never fully convey that amazing place to anyone he knew, but every piece of archaeological evidence that came to light would help build up a better picture than we would otherwise have.

He sat through lessons and ran around the playground as though nothing had happened, which as far as he knew it hadn't, but meanwhile the letters had made an impact on the ‘Time Team’ production crew. Some of the team were against doing anything because they were already snowed under with interesting places to dig, but a few felt that it would be silly not to make a few inquiries at least. Eventually, it was agreed that they would go over to the building site and try and talk to someone.

The local paper came out on Thursday and carried a front page article about David's school's petition to ‘Time Team’, with photographs of David holding up the pile of letters in front of Channel 4 HQ and another picture of the building site in the City. The article reminded people that David was already a celebrated junior archaeologist, and went on to mention the Museum of London curator, and talk about his appearance on the news when he had nearly been assaulted by a fellow archaeologist. David chuckled as he recalled the professor being dragged out of the TV studio after he had been denounced as a fraud. David knew the truth, but the Professor really wasn't a very nice man, and anyway, how could David explain that it was all a misunderstanding because he had travelled back in time?

On Thursday in school, a reporter from the London Evening Standard came to the school. He knew David as well, having covered the story of David's coin find, and he was here to get more information about the article that had appeared in the local paper. He spent a long time with the head-teacher and asked David a few questions as well. After he got some pictures, he headed off, mentioning that he was going over to the building site and to Channel 4 as well.

The final edition of the Standard had a detailed article, although it was on the inside pages and there was no picture of David. Instead, there was a stock picture of Tony Robinson and another of the building site, with a picture of David's coins inset.

The article began,

> **DON'T BURY OUR PAST**
> LONDON SCHOOL ASK TIME TEAM
> **'PLEASE SAVE OUR CITY HERITAGE'**
>
> Children from a Tower Hamlets School have written hundreds of letters to Channel 4's Time Team programme asking them to step in to save a possible archaeological site before builders move in. …

It went on at length, and David was excited to read that the team had spoken to the contractors and persuaded them to allow a brief geophysical survey to be carried out to see if there might be anything of interest. The contractors were apparently, 'very concerned about Britain's heritage and had the interests of science and historians high on their list of priorities'. David thought this was not really true but he didn't mind, if it meant they might find the time capsule he had buried with Marcus.

Friday was the last day of term and all anyone could talk about in school was their petition. That evening, the local South East news carried a short item about the story, and the newsreader read out statements from the contractors and from a Channel 4 spokesperson.

On Saturday, David got a call from his head-teacher. 'Time Team' had invited them all over to the building site where they thought they had found something potentially interesting in the geophysical survey.

A representative of the contractor was there, and several people from Channel 4, and even Tony Robinson was there, which David guessed must mean there was something really important going on.

They showed the results of the geophysical survey, which just looked like fuzzy nonsense and loads of writing to David, but they explained that there was clearly evidence of possible archaeology that might be interesting, and several features that could justify putting in some trenches.

The TV crew's legal experts had got a ruling allowing them access to the site for a dig during the coming week, which the contractor claimed, through gritted teeth, was a good decision and in the interests of the furtherance of knowledge.

There were camera crews, and sound engineers, and volunteers arriving, as well as various 'Time Team' presenters and experts, many of whom were familiar faces to David.

Within the first few hours of digging they got very excited, as they uncovered some post holes but these turned out to be part of a Saxon building from the 6th century.

As the day wore on, more trenches were put in at various places across the site, there were numerous small finds, including establishing that a part of the London Wall cut across one corner of the site. This proved, beyond any shadow of doubt, that the entire site lay outside the City limits, which was a bit of a blow.

IX
IN A BLACK BOX

The following day there were several more finds, although not all were from the Roman period, and most were small and not very significant. On the third day, Tony Robinson was in front of the cameras saying "It's day three and we've found nothing to show that this is an important Roman site. Perhaps we shouldn't be surprised because we now know for sure that we are outside the original Roman wall. We're hoping that today will reveal more but we aren't holding our breath."

It was getting late on the Monday when there was a shout from one of the trenches. One of the volunteers had hit a stone slab and had to stop while the experts came over to investigate. As the slab was revealed, painstakingly removing mud and stones with the most delicate touch, it became clear that it was a monument of some sort.

The whole process took ages, far longer than it ever took when David was watching on the television at home. It rained and tarpaulins were stretched over the trench billowing in the breeze as the diggers scraped and brushed and teased the centuries old stones out of the surrounding heavy clay.

Eventually they revealed a small burial chamber. There was an inscription

DIS MANIB
M SEPTIMUS FABER
VIXIT ANNIS LXII
VET - PATER - FABRIC
H F C

Phil explained,

“We know it's a tomb because of the inscription. The first line is an abbreviation of Dis Manibus. It is addressed to the spirits of the dead. Then we have the name ‘M(arcus) Septimus Faber. 'Vixit Annis LXII' so he lived to the ripe old age of sixty-two which was a good innings in Roman times, especially when you see 'VET' which doesn't mean he cared for sick animals, it means he was a soldier. 'Pater' is father and 'Fabric' I reckon means he was a builder or something? 'H F C' is an abbreviation meaning his heir had this tomb made."

After a little while longer, they uncovered a small urn which would have contained the remains of David's old friend after his cremation. David felt a bit silly because he wanted to cry. Logically he knew that Marcus was dead. He lived one thousand eight hundred years ago. But seeing his tomb and the urn like that made it all real.

Close to the urn was another item that the archaeologists were not expecting. A small box made of wood and covered in lead sheeting was carefully extracted and investigated. There was a tense few minutes as the box was opened, and inside they found a variety of unrelated items, coins, beads, a small pot, a comb, a broach, sewing needles, a writing stylus.

There was a great deal of discussion about this item because nobody had really seen anything quite like it before. It was just a simple box containing a variety of everyday items. Phil Harding explained to Tony Robinson

"There are no high status objects here, it's the Roman equivalent of someone today putting a load of common items like pens, cheap costume jewelery, that sort of thing, along with some small change, into a sealed container and burying them as if they were grave goods."

"Like a sort of Roman time capsule?" enthused Tony.

"Exactly like a time capsule." agreed Phil. "But I've never seen anything like this in any Roman burial before. We may not have discovered a palace or a temple, but we've certainly uncovered something that will keep scholars talking for a while to come."

And with that Tony Robinson did a piece to camera summing up the three days events, and crew members started packing things away.

In the trench, a couple of young archaeologists from London University who were at the dig, getting some hands on experience, were still having a bit of a nose around the tomb, and one of them pulled some items out of the clay. After a bit of gentle cleaning, the items turned out to be a pair of reading glasses and a small metal spirit level. One of the students chuckled and held the items out to his friend,

"Hey, do you think I should rush over and tell them about this?" he asked, with a wink.

"Umm, maybe best not to, unless you want to make a proper twit of yourself like our old professor, with his marble necklace!" replied the other student.

"Ha ha, that was hilarious, did you see him on T.V. when the security guards had to drag him from the studio?"

They both laughed, packed up their tools and hurried to follow the rest of the crew.

David was a bit disappointed that he could not go into school to enjoy this new glory, but he did at least have another newspaper interview, and his photo was in the local paper again. It was now the summer holidays, and he was looking forward to going away for a couple of weeks to the seaside.

Archaeology would just have to take second place to ice creams, fish and chips, and sandcastles; at least until the autumn term.

NOTES – N.B.

N.B. stands for nota bene which means note well. It is one of many things we get from the Romans, along with about half of all English words, and a huge amount of our culture. The Romans occupied Britain for nearly four hundred years from 43 AD to 410 AD so it is hardly surprising that they had a lot of influence.

A few things in the text may be unfamiliar to some. The Gherkin is the nickname of a famous building, 30 St Mary Axe, in London which is shaped more like a huge cigar than a pickled vegetable. There are several Celtic myths about people visiting the land of the Gods. In the stories they often spend only a short time there, but when they return time has passed very quickly. This is why David's friend believes he has gone to that land and returned.

This book is a sequel to Time Tunnel to Londinium and David goes back to a slightly different time, about fifty years later than his first visit. This period of Roman British history was a bit more troubled and it is thought that London Wall was built because of that. Archaeologists still don't know exactly when the wall was built and of course, we don't know the names of the engineers or craftsmen who worked on it.

One of the reasons why archaeology is so important is because it helps us to piece together stories from ancient times. Often there are conflicts between science and commerce but not always; and it is not always the scientists who are right. You have to try and get both sides of the story and then make your own mind up.

David's campaign of letter writing was very effective, and indeed getting a petition together is often a good way to highlight an important issue in real life as well. Try it some-time.

ABOUT THE AUTHOR

Olli Tooley is a father of four who has spent the best part of his life trying to avoid doing any proper work. He was the lead singer in 'Led Zep Too' (a Led Zeppelin tribute band) for seven years during which time he sang in front of audiences ranging from a few folks who just came in from the rain, to thousands of screaming rock fans. Olli was also briefly in a reformed version of The Honeycombs with one original member.

He wrote a 1500 word contribution to The Great Explorers by Robin Hanbury-Tenison ISBN-13: 978-0500251690 and has a number of websites on various topics.

He has also had a go at everything from selling life insurance to office and domestic removals, and selling tents and rucksacks in camping shops to being a London private hire driver.

He now lives in North Devon, where he divides his time between doing odd jobs, writing, political activism, and correcting people's grammar on social media.

55309080R00042

Made in the USA
Charleston, SC
25 April 2016